This book belongs to

. . . .

For Ava
With love from Mummy.

ISBN 978 1 4052 2753 7 (Hardback)
ISBN 978 1 4052 2754 4 (Paperback)

10 9 8 7 6 5 4 3 2 1

A CIP catalogue record for this title
is available from
The British Library

Text and illustrations copyright © Lydia Monks 2007

Lydia Monks has asserted
her moral rights

Printed in Singapore

First published in
Great Britain in 2007
by Egmont UK Limited,
239 Kensington High Street,
London W8 6SA

EGMONT

We bring stories to life

Gorilla!

LYDIA MONKS

EGMONT

Hurrah! My friend had arrived at last!
He had come to stay with me for a few days.
I was excited, and he was excited too.

"Ooo, ooo, OOO!"
I think he was going to like it.

We'd bought lots of food we thought he would like,
and cooked a meal especially for him.

We had banana broth,

followed by
banana burgers,

with banoffee pie
for dessert.

"Ooo, ooo, ooo!"
he said.
I think he liked it.

When we went to bed, I let him have the top bunk. I thought he'd feel more at home there.

"Ooo, ooo, OOO!"
he said as he snuggled up for the night.
I think he liked it.

Overnight it had snowed.
He had never seen snow before.

He licked it,

poked it,

tasted it,

and sat in it,
before he said,
"Ooo, ooo, ooo!"

I think he liked it.

We thought we would take him out
for the day and do lots of snowy things.

First we took him skiing.
We thought he'd like that.

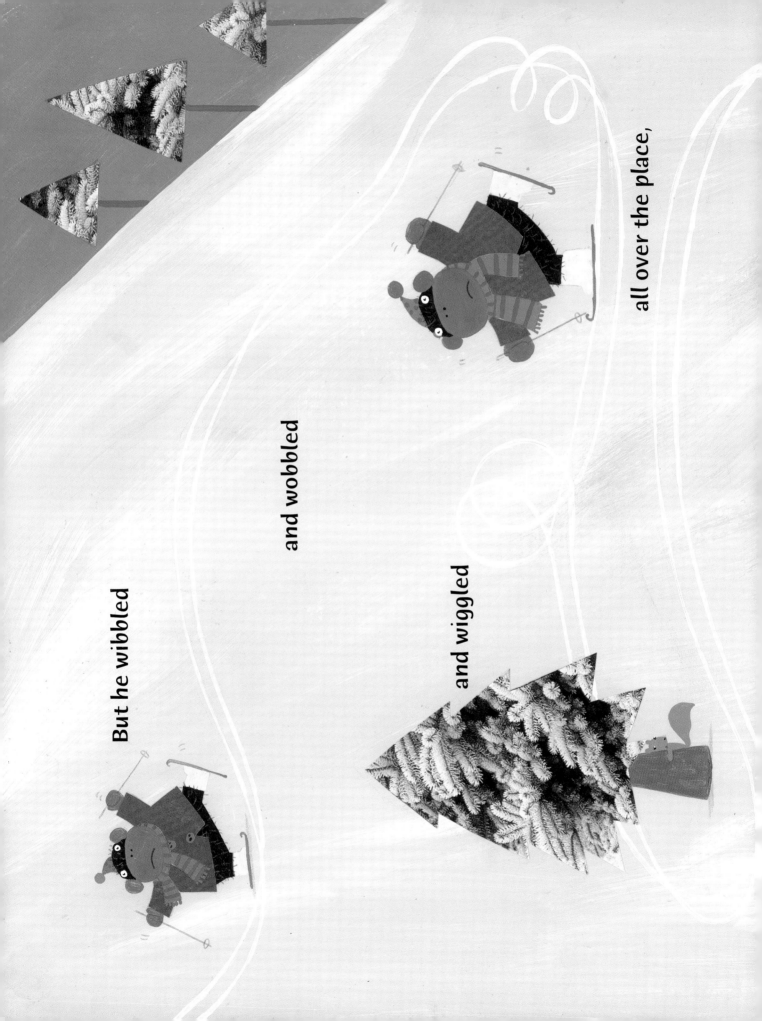

But he wibbled

and wobbled

and wiggled

all over the place,

until he toppled over

and rolled all the way

down the ski slope.

"Ooo, ooo, ooo!" he moaned.

I don't think he liked it.

So we took him skating.
We thought he would like that.

But he wibbled

and wobbled

and wiggled
all over the place
until . . .

. . . he slipped and fell with a big bump on his **big bottom.**

"Ooo, ooo, ooo!" he groaned.

I don't think he liked it.

By this time, Gorilla was feeling very sorry for himself,
so we took him off to make snowmen.

We thought he'd like that.

But his snowman wibbled

and wobbled
and wiggled
all over the place until . . .

. . . it fell right on top of him!
"Ooo, ooo, ooo!" he cried.

He *didn't* like it.

I wondered how to make him feel better.
Then I thought of something . . .

"There must be lots of things you *are* good at," I said.
"I bet you're good at swinging!"

With that, Gorilla smiled.
He lifted me up onto
his back and started
to climb the nearest tree.

Then he swung . . .

. . . and we wibbled

and wobbled

and wiggled

all over the place . . .

But then our **Ooo, ooo, ooos** turned into
Hoo, hoo, hoos! and **Ha, ha, hahs!**
He was laughing, and I was laughing, too.

He **DID** like it!

Gorilla felt so much better. He decided to have just one more try at skiing, and skating, and making a snowman.

And although he still wibbled and wobbled and wiggled, he just kept on laughing.

"Ooo, **ooo, OOO,** Hoo, **hoo, hoo,** Ha, **ha, ha!**"

And I kept on laughing too.

I was a bit sad when it was time
for Gorilla to go home,

but I *knew* we would be seeing him again soon.

Next time it would be our turn to visit and . . .

. . . Ooo, ooo, ooo!

I knew I was going to like it!

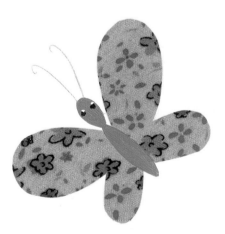

ENJOY MORE BRILLIANT BOOKS BY Lydia

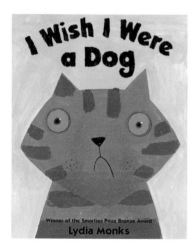

Winner of the Smarties Bronze Award

I Wish I Were a Dog

Kitty is fed up with being a cat.
Dogs have all the fun.
But then she finds out that maybe
being a cat isn't so bad after all.

ISBN 978 14052 1246 5 (paperback)
ISBN 978 14052 1751 4 (board book)

Aaaarrgghh, Spider!

All Spider wants is to belong
to a family. The trouble is,
she SCARES everyone too much!
Poor Spider. How will she ever
get people to like her?

ISBN 978 14052 1044 7 (paperback)
ISBN 978 14052 2319 5 (board book)
ISBN 978 14052 3044 5 (book and audio)

No More Eee-Orrh!

Dicky Donkey drives everyone crazy!
Each morning they wake up to
eE**E-Orrh!** eE**E-Orrh!**
All the neighbours want to send him away,
until the day **Dicky Donkey** loses
his voice all together and is rushed to
the animal hospital.
Suddenly they miss him!

ISBN 978 14052 1740 8 (paperback)
ISBN 978 14052 2919 7 (board book)